Unruly Mix I: Tales of Music, Artists, Posers and Misfits

By Bob Deakin

Bob Deakin

Copyright 2026

Bob Deakin

Illustrations by John Coutinho

Cover by Walter H. Von Egidy

Cover image used courtesy of Maurice Zetina

No part of this book may be used or reproduced in any manner whatsoever without written permission except in the case of brief quotations embodied in critical articles and reviews.

Those events are drawn from the author's imagination, and not to be construed as real. Any opinions expressed are those of the narrator or the characters, and not the author, so you can blame them.

Tales of Music, Artists, Posers and Misfits

Dedicated to Mom and Susie

Contents

1 Redneck Notary Public 6

2 School Play Sucks........12

3 Unruly Mix........20

4 All Caught Up in the Reverie........25

5 You and Me Against the World........31

6 Rest Stop Sally 37

7 Runners Are Dicks 45

8 Don't Go Near the Water........54

9 Soccer Whore........59

10 Creep Filter........64

11 Hispanic Meghan 71

12 What's with the Long Ass? 77

13 I Met This Amazing Writer........82

14 Covid Chic........91

15 The Six Degrees of Christmas........100

16 Poets with Stupid Names I........106

17 Poets with Stupid Names II 112

18 Frankie's Studio........118

19 Straw Hat Weirdo........123

20 Afternoon Delight 130

21 A-Hole in the Fedora 138

22 Tip Your Bartender 146

About the Author 154

1
Redneck Notary Public

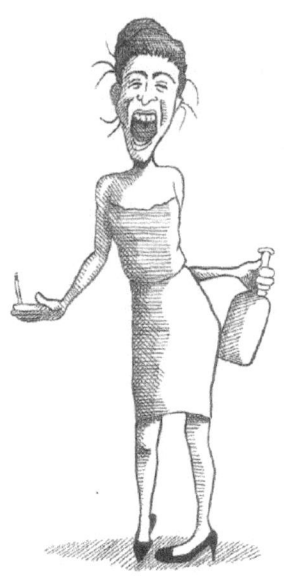

There's fun and there's sick, and this party is sick.

Stacey Gillen received her notary public certification from the state of Florida today and it is party time tonight at the Hard Times Tavern in her hometown of Burnham, Connecticut.

Stacey put a *good* couple days into becoming a notary, especially since her boss requested that she become one to save the company more than $200 a year.

She came. She did. She is a notary, and no one can take that away from her except for the state if she doesn't pay her $39 bonding fee.

This is no small task in Stacey's life. After a grueling hour-long application and several days of emails and writing samples requiring that she type full words and sentences, she did it. It's not the first test she's taken since high school but the first she's completed.

Stacey is a notary; stamp and all. She's aware of the badass reputation notaries have for their reckless lifestyles but it will not define her. She is so much more than a name on paper, although at $10 per, hers is one of the most expensive signatures in town.

As a Florida notary, she may charge up to $10 for any 'notarial act' and up to $30 as a 'wedding officiant.' It is a fact not lost on her or the $25 bottle of whiskey she drinks from this evening, raising a toast to her friends.

"This is for everybody that thought I could never do nothin'," Stacey barked to the crowd of 20 friends, all visibly intoxicated upon arrival at Hard Times. "Cheers crackheads!"

I eventually make my way through the smoke and crowd to congratulate her and take a photo in case my editor is interested in running a story about a small-town girl's accomplishment. She tries to explain what a notary does but is too hammered, so I look it up on my phone.

A notary must be bonded ($7,500 in Florida) in the state which they are licensed. There are Basic and Standard Notary agents in addition to Complete Notary agents, which require a higher level of training and more expensive exam.

Stacey's good with being a Basic for now though she vows to go for the top level as soon as she saves up the $260 for the exam.

"I ain't foolin' around with this," she says to me after a long pull off her Jack Daniels bottle. "Once I get that I'm looking at running for public office."

There was no mention of which office, only that she wants to make a difference in some way for something, somewhere, for some reason.

Requirements for a notary in Florida stipulate that you are at least 18 years-old, a legal resident of the state, can understand, read and write English and that you have not been convicted of a felony. Stacey just squeaks in on the latter two. She tried to become a notary in Connecticut, but the application process proved too rigorous and requirements too stringent.

According to *National Notary Monthly* - a notorious page turner for those in the industry - new notaries receive an official notary seal stamp, a softcover notary journal with tamper-proof, Smyth-sewn binding and a Notary Public sign, which is as effective as a home security sign except it warns intruders that the crime will be officially documented.

Her friends spray her with champagne before I light her cigarette as she bathes in the adoration. She proudly brags she can now officially declare somebody an asshole.

"Any y'all burnouts wanna mess with me now goin' get written up with the state," she shouts while blowing out smoke and wiping her nose. "I'll go notary on your ass!"

She doesn't yet realize that her notary license is not valid in Connecticut, but she spends every spring in the Sunshine State and feels she identifies with the lifestyles of many Floridians. In the meantime, she has plenty of friends up north who have nice things to say about her on this special occasion.

"She always had a lovely signature," attests her Aunt Peggy, taking the edge off with a triple bourbon and coke as she grooves to a Lynyrd Skynyrd song on the dance floor.

"When she wanna do somethin' ain't nobody goin' stop her," assured a glassy-eyed Daryl Dooley, who claims he dated Stacey when she was 15. "You goin' be readin' about her someday."

2
School Play Sucks

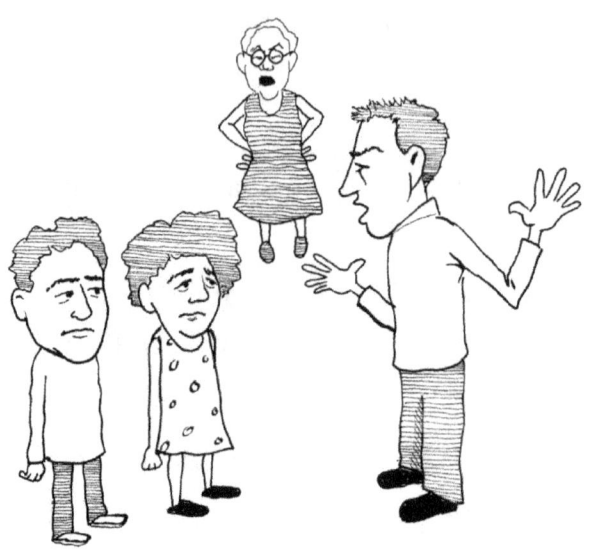

Students at Curtis Elementary School are distressed after learning a hard life lesson on Tuesday night. At the school assembly, hosted by the self-described "new thinking" individuals on the Burnham Board of Education, it was divulged that the school musical, scheduled for its opening performance on Friday, is not up to par.

"It sucks," said clearly resentful science teacher Michael Tuzman about the play. He directed the annual school musical at Curtis for 22 years until Language Arts Teacher Steven Gabriel took over for him last year.

"I'm glad nobody but parents ever show up for the show because taxpayers would be appalled at where their dollars are going," Mr. Tuzman added to a rousing ovation.

The musical, *Anything Goes*, is a standard in community theater, schools, and chock-full of classic songs by Cole Porter. It first opened on Broadway in 1934 starring stage legend Ethel Merman.

"I knew Ethel Merman, and you're no Ethel Merman," stated grandparent Hedy LaFrance, who spoke at the assembly, pointing to 11-year-old Kayla Lang, who plays Hope Harcourt, the female lead.

According to several students interviewed after the assembly, Ms. LaFrance has been attending rehearsals, walking around as if she is the director and criticizing cast members for not displaying the passion of a professional.

Asked to respond, Ms. LaFrance disputed any claims of interference, stating that the director requested her assistance. She was a clothing designer for the New York City stage in the 1960s and 70s and haughtily assures she "knows a thing or two" about the theater, or *theatre* as she pronounces it.

She worked with Ms. Merman on several Broadway productions and could see right away that Ms. Lang "should focus on schoolwork" regarding career aspirations.

"Broadway wasn't paved with good intentions," boomed Burnham Mayor, Phil Stewart, to the cast members, who cowered in one corner of the auditorium. "If you weren't spendin' so much time on them damn computers, maybe you'd have time for some learnin'. Try typin' 'THIS MUSICAL SUCKS' into one o' them Internet search things and dog-gonnit if 'CURTIS ELEMENTARY SCHOOL' don't pop up first."

Mr. Stewart's theory was quickly blown by a student with a smart phone when Andrew Lloyd Webber's *Cats* appeared first, but his point was well made, if not well taken.

Annabella Wagner, whose ten-year-old son plays Moonface Martin, pointed out that a shortened version of the play or perhaps a different musical altogether might be more appropriate for students, who range in age from 5-to-12.

"How about *Godspell* or *Little Shop of Horrors*," she supposed. "A few songs, easy sets and costumes and a plot that leaves room for kids to improvise."

"This isn't the eighties anymore, Annabella," responded parent Shondra Hipp, an alumna of the school with Ms. Wagner. "That was fine when our parents and teachers were smoking P.O.T., even more than you and I were, but we can't get away with that stuff anymore."

Conversation then shifted toward the budget and how vital it is they show the county that an elementary school can stage a sophisticated musical, and that talent presented is an incentive for more funding to arts education.

"And the Covid outbreak showed us that online learning works for everyone, right?" chirped Loretta Coppola, a brash second grade teacher who has seen students ridiculed in class for participating in the production. "*Anything Goes* is too much for children. This production sucks and the students suck, but at least they are trying and should be commended for that.

"I find it oddly coincidental, however, that Mr. Gabriel chose a show featuring the song 'Blow, Gabriel, Blow,'" she added. "Is there another message here?"

Twelve-year-old Tate Bailey, who plays the male lead, Billy Crocker, was not a happy sixth grader upon hearing the review of his performance by music teacher Emily Kravec, who also spoke at the assembly, scolding students she described as "immature" and "unfocused." She worked briefly with Bailey until taking a leave of absence from her post for personal reasons.

"My uncle said he once slept over at Misses Kravec's house, but she always acts quiet when I tell her uncle Steve says hello," said Bailey, the wise-beyond-his-years youngster in an interview later that evening.

Bailey, a straight-D student and nephew of the director, feels students and teachers at Curtis are sabotaging his musical pursuits.

He sat steaming in his seat at the assembly as accusations flew.

"Everybody knows Caleb Canfield shoulda' got the part," shouted nine-year-old Wendy Slayton, who plays Bonnie in the production. "Tate was in Special Ed until fifth-grade. He's one of the stupid kids. I heard Mister Gabriel just wants him to feel good about himself because his dad used to beat him up."

Rifts quickly developed between Bailey and other members of the production during rehearsals. He and Chorus Teacher Neil Gabel nearly came to blows at a high-tension rehearsal Monday. Mr. Gabel was coaching him through voice inflections used by singers of the 1920s and 30s when Bailey was reluctant to follow along with an old recording of "Mammy."

Still hot over the dispute, Bailey feels he's done nothing wrong.

"He wants me to sing all these stupid songs from 200 hundred years ago," said the sixth grader after the assembly, taking a long pull off his Marlboro. "What am I? Al-fuckin-Jolson?"

3
Unruly Mix

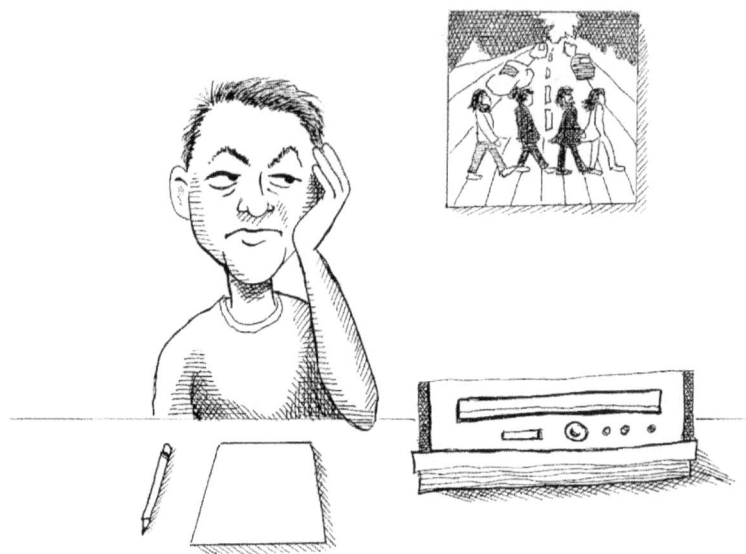

Dear D.E. Conover,

    You do not know me, but I feel compelled to write to you regarding the cassette player I just purchased at a tag sale in Burnham, Connecticut. I found your Eustis, Florida, name tag and address inside of it when I started cleaning the tape heads and oiling the rollers.

It is a beautiful deck. Nakamichis were some of the best available in the mid-80s when this was manufactured. Looks like you took good care of it, too, and for that I thank you very much. Quite forward thinking of you to put your name on it in case it was ever lost or stolen, which I hope is not the case as I intend to keep it.

The reason I am writing is because of the cassette you apparently left in the deck. It was a mix tape you must have made a long time ago and I have listened to it many times and am impressed with the musical selections. It's not every day I hear Eddy Arnold doing a Motown song or an Ella Fitzgerald and Mel Torme duet.

What does not impress me is the ebb and flow of your unruly mix of songs. Early on Side A you follow Jose Feliciano's "Light My Fire" with Elvin Bishop's "Fooled Around and Fell in Love." These two songs could not be any more different in feel, construction, style or fidelity. One recording is a Spanish-styled, acoustic guitar-driven ballad while the other is pure blues rock.

What were you thinking?

Another combination I have a problem with is Richard Harris's "MacArthur Park" followed by Seals & Crofts "Diamond Girl." An Irish actor singing a dramatic, lyrically confusing love song followed by an American duo known for their ultra-new age religious beliefs? Seriously?

Bad segue and it detracts from the quintessentially American 70s sunshine feel of the Seals & Crofts piece.

Late on Side B you made the awkward decision to include Ronnie Milsap's "It Was Almost Like a Song" followed by Barbara Mandrell's "(If Loving You is Wrong) I Don't Want to be Right."

Emotional confusion anyone?

First, the Luther Ingram version of "(If Loving You) …" holds ten times the emotional impact over the Mandrell version, but I will give you a pass in that Mandrell's country sensibilities work better on your tape. The two songs should not follow one another, however, in that Milsap laments a genuinely innocent lost love while Mandrell selfishly brags of an illicit affair that everyone should be ashamed of, including you for putting the two songs back-to-back on your tape.

I'll keep the criticisms to a minimum. The quality of the tape was good and living in Eustis in the 80s surrounded by orange groves, pickup trucks and Richard Petty fans, you must have had a lot of free time to over-think the choreography of your mix.

I will hold onto the tape if you don't mind but if you want it back, send me an email or self-addressed stamped envelope and I will put it in the mail. I can even, dare I say, burn a disk or file of it if you want, but the audio levels of your mix are so dynamically inconsistent that I fear the analog to digital conversion will sound discordant on your computer, phone, Victrola or whatever contraption you listen to music on these days.

I wish you the best of luck and thank you again for taking good care of this deck. I get the impression you are a nice person and I think we are kindred spirits in our musical tastes. The Nakamichi is great and will sound even better with some maintenance and more sensitivity to musical selections.

Sincerely,

Seth from Kent, CT

P.S.: Next time, more than one second between songs. A more dramatic pause makes for better listening, and the music search feature requires at least two seconds to work properly.

Tales of Music, Artists, Posers and Misfits

4
All Caught Up in the Reverie

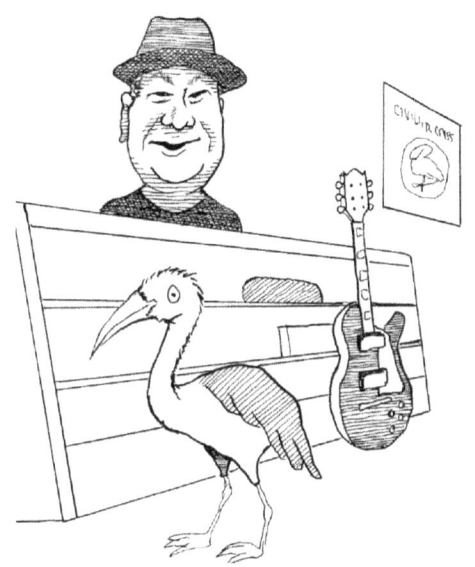

Sailing takes me away to where I've always heard it could be.

Every time I see a flamingo, I think of Christopher Cross's tremendously successful self-titled album and smash hit song,

"Sailing," from 1980. The cover features an illustrated pink flamingo, placidly perched on one leg in the middle of a pond, encircled in a dark green frame. I remember it on the floor of many living rooms at the time, usually leaning against an entertainment system, having recently been played.

Why I remember this is because the album was so mellow, and as a young aspiring reporter, I took note that the most unlikely of characters had it in their possession. My sisters had it, and I could understand that, but my brothers too, and they were more into Pink Floyd or The Stones.

We lived near the Burnham volunteer fire department, and even some of the biggest, toughest guys could be seen with the album or cassette in their truck or in the saddlebag of their motorcycle. I even saw the flamingo album under the arm of the occasional classmate in school, which blew me away seeing as how image conscious middle school students were and always have been.

This album was a bellwether for other albums often spotted at the homes of people under the age of 40 at the time and for years after. Steely Dan's *Gaucho* was one, although most people who had that one were too coked up to listen to it.

Here are some other culprits:

The Long Run by The Eagles suffered the same fate as *Gaucho*, but FM radio program directors had an easier time convincing their DJs to play a few more tracks from this one. If music fans were doing drugs while listening to *The Long Run*, that was okay, but apparently with *Gaucho* they had to look a little harder to find someone else on the same page.

Breakfast in America by Supertramp. People didn't have to be high on anything to enjoy this album. If they were, though, no problem. It was cool to not like this one back then, but you could count on finding it in whatever home you visited, like wood paneling and shag carpeting.

52nd Street by Billy Joel was hot with enduring success from its release the previous year. "Big Shot" was the hit at the time, which may have been the first point at which some of the radio listening public realized it was getting a little *too* much of Billy Joel.

The *Christopher Cross* album appealed to such a broad audience first and foremost for the entrancing melody of "Sailing," but it featured some of the hottest musicians of the time including Michael McDonald, Don Henley, guitar legends Larry Carlton and Eric Johnson as well as vocalists Nicolette Larson and J.D. Souther. It also had a hard-driving rock tune in "Ride Like the Wind," which made its way into other genres including NASCAR and the NBA as a song for highlight films.

I listened to the album beginning to end many times and always thought it was rather forgettable save for the two hits. I loved "Ride Like the Wind" for its steady thumping drum part (I could almost play it on drums) and the smoking guitar solo at the end (I couldn't play it on guitar). Speaking of which, with Larry Carlton and Eric Johnson booked for the sessions, why would Christopher Cross play the guitar solo on this track, as he is credited? In any event, he nailed it.

I will admit I always loved the song "Sailing" (I nailed the triangle part) and its mesmerizing, rudimentary guitar rhythm as the main verse. The entire track has a lot of 'air' in it, enabling the listener to hear every strike of every note. The piano solo subtly arrives more than halfway through and carries this peaceful journey on an alternate course before gently settling back to the original theme and 'not far back to sanity.'

As a boy at the time, I was stuck on John Lennon's *Double Fantasy*, as well as the resurgence of the older country music artists. Although I grew to love "Sailing," I had my doubts about Christopher Cross's album when it came out because I hadn't heard of him. He didn't look like a rock star as much as he did the guy behind the deli counter, and again with that pink flamingo cover.

I'd be willing to bet Warner Brothers had doubts about the cover too, which may have pushed them over the edge to spring for the session fees of McDonald, Henley and the others. On another note, looking at the back of the album, I don't see any members of Toto credited. Is it possible there was an album from this period on which none of them played? I have my suspicions.

As it turns out, it seems I was the only one afraid to flaunt my affection for this album, but I bet there were others. "Sailing" was taking everyone else away to where they always heard it would be, I just wasn't all caught up in the reverie.

5
You and Me Against the World

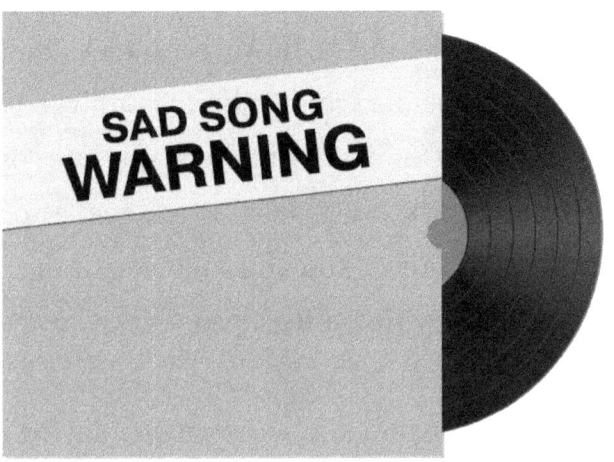

I was always a sucker for a good heart-rending song from the 1970s.

When I was a little kid roaming the shores of lakes and streams, my only cares in the world were finding rocks to skim across the water and hoping my brothers and sisters would let me stop by their rooms and listen to music. They were into Chicago, Led Zeppelin, Blue Oyster Cult and everything else, and I was hip to the music scene except for things like how The Doobie Brothers got their name.

I did have some of my own forbidden musical pleasures, however, such as Bread, The Carpenters and Gilbert O'Sullivan (yes, Gilbert O'Sullivan) but there was one song I adored, which was just too sad to play on the family stereo: "You and Me Against the World," by Helen Reddy.

I remember it occasionally playing in the house, typically followed by a universal sense of melancholy or someone pulling it off the turntable for something more upbeat.

The song was written by Paul Williams and Kenny Ascher and sadly emotes a single mother's plight 'against the world' and how they will 'muddle through' when 'one of us is left to carry on' and so forth.

It also included the line 'how you were frightened by the clown,' which was one of the first mainstream references to clown fright before it became chic in the 1980s with lactose intolerance, food allergies and attention deficit disorder.

It is an amazingly beautiful song. A small orchestra counterbalances the melody with stunning vibrato electric guitar and ever-so-subtle harmonica fills while Helen works her magic on the lead vocal. For added anguish, Helen's young daughter is included in the mix, cooing "I love you mommy" at the end for maximum melodrama.

The little bastard.

The song's sentiment fits any situation at a given time of impossible odds or sadness and unfortunately works well for those looking to be sad. Someone in the house bought the record not long after it was released in 1974 and I played it a few times, but it was just too sad, and I wouldn't play it in front of anyone for fear that I might tear up. The notes were sad enough on their own but to hear the lyrics was just too much.

That didn't, however, stop me from playing it hundreds of times in the ensuing years, captivated by the melody and the impossibly poignant lyrics buttressing my mood at a particular moment in time.

"You and Me Against the World" always hit me hard. I wanted to be independent like most kids and occasionally had 'me against the world' feelings in a negative way so I identified with the lyrics. At the same time, I was captivated with the notes and the musical performance in a positive way, creating a powerful emotional collision to ruin a good afternoon.

I must add that at the time, I still had the wonderful innocence to believe that songs were 'real' in the sense that the singer was telling their own true story. This caused me to wrestle with the dichotomy: If you're Helen Reddy – beautiful, rich and famous – aren't things going better than that for you these days?

I always wondered what the inspiration for the song was, so, being a good reporter, I decided to go to the source and contact Paul Williams.

"It's one of those songs that seems to resonate with single parents," he said, praising the late Helen Reddy for her performance. "I get a lot of nice 'heart payments' from people thanking me for the song. It's the best part of being a songwriter. Thanks for honoring the tune."

I didn't tell him I'm not actually 'honoring' the tune but now that I think about it I am. It is a brilliant work and stops me in my tracks whenever I hear it.

One final source of sweet torment is the message the song leaves implanted in my soul, which is to remember the tough times and those who helped you through it.

> *Then remembering will have to do,*
> *Our memories alone will get us through.*
> *Think about the days of me and you,*
> *You and me against the world*

To those who have never been through tough times, no problem. To those who have, I can get you the name of a good therapist.

I didn't ask Mr. Williams if he was trying to burden the listener with that message but I have a growing list of concerns about the song that just might warrant another call.

Damn you Paul Williams and Kenny Ascher.

6
Rest Stop Sally

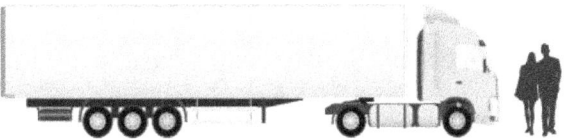

Traveling has brought me to a lot of highway rest stops. In all that time I've encountered many shady characters, from people who stop there to people who work there to people who live there.

One character I recently discovered I never knew existed until I pulled into a rest stop along the Interstate and someone pointed her out: Rest Stop Sally.

Sally is a woman of questionable morals though not a woman of ill repute. She likes to hang around rest stops looking for Mr. Right for the night. He may not be nice, he may not be right, but he may be hers for the night.

Meet Rest Stop John.

Rest Stop Sally doesn't care. She doesn't want money, she's just looking for a little peace, love and understanding. What's so funny about that?

Sally is a woman confused. She knows better than to troll a rest stop for love, but knowledge vanishes when she pulls off the highway. It is a state of confusion no woman should ever find herself in, and no one would want for her, but Sally is in a bad place, in more ways than one.

She's looking for a diamond in the rough, and only the rough will find her. There are plenty of nice men that stop here but she won't find any because none of them will let themselves find her.

"Hi," I say to 'Sally' as I have no choice but to pass her on the way to the restroom. I keep my head down and move swiftly to avoid a conversation. Nonetheless, I feel for her and wish she would just get in her car and leave this place in her rear-view mirror.

"Hey honey, how you doin?" she replies.

"Good, thanks. Nice rest area, huh?" I joke. "Looks a lot like all the other ones."

The conversation goes no further although she wants to talk. I cannot get away fast enough.

Just minutes before, it was the security guard who told me she calls herself Lil, but everyone knows her as Rest Stop Sally. An employee of the state for years, he knows her routine well.

Sally's evening goes something like this: She wanders around the vending machines and restrooms looking to strike up a conversation with the most normal looking guy wandering the area. Occasionally, she finds one, usually a trucker looking for a friend to solve the world's problems.

She might not have a lot to offer in the way of solutions but is willing to try, and for that she gains friends easily. Everyone likes Sally, and Sally deserves respect, whether she gets it or not.

If she is going to be a Rest Stop Sally, then there are going to be Rest Stop Johns. A human lost and found depository it is. None of them want to be here but they all have been left behind, in one way or another, and are looking to find something, whether they know what it is or not.

It's a vicious cycle, one that avails itself just off the highway, so far from home, and so close to their lonely hearts.

Meet Duane.

Duane's been on the road for days in his semi with sleeper cab and is desperate for a friend. A long spell on the road will do that and Duane has no friends to begin with so he's noticeably lonely. He is the only man in his own world and in Sally he sees Miss America.

While he's the man of most people's nightmares, Sally is the girl of his dreams. It's been a few days since he showered but he's got enough gift of gab to get by and that's enough for her.

"Oh, I can never find anything I want here," Sally says, crouching in front of the vending machine, making a pose for Duane, who is approaching a few feet away.

"Whatya lookin' for pretty lady?" he responds. She turns to him with a little smile and a fake look of frustration with the selections.

"Something better than a candy bar," she replies, coyly looking back at the machine.

"Ain't gonna find much more in that thing," he says with a friendly laugh. "Where you comin' from?"

"Virginia. It's been a long day and I'm hungry and tired."

"I know the feelin'. Set down a minute and take a load off," he says with conviction.

It goes from there until Sally has had an evening to talk about the next morning, where she remains at the same rest stop.

Is she a better woman today? No. Is she happy? No. Is it the next day? Yes. That's all that matters. As Kris Kristofferson wrote, Duane helped her make it through the night.

Duane's on the road again and feeling great on this bright new day. Sally doesn't feel the same but doesn't care. He's singing to the Marshall Tucker Band on his way to South Carolina. She catches herself on a bench without a mate.

It's not a happy story but rest stops are not happy places. Everyone is there because they can't stand the road anymore.

Sally's not the only one to make the rest stop her home away from home. There's Rest Stop Brucie, who is looking for a completely different variety of illicit thrill. And there's Rest Stop Bojangles, who makes his home from stop to stop, in worn out shoes.

Sally decides to get back on the road to wherever inspiration takes her. She's planning to visit her sister in Maine but beyond that who knows. She hopes for inspiration or a pleasant surprise. Maybe both.

"Ride, Sally Ride," is the mantra she sings to herself as she makes her way to her old Toyota Camry with a change of clothes and a few possessions in the back. The car is cold from an autumn night in the lot. As she clicks the remote to unlock it, she notices an old Mustang parked next to her with a male silhouette in the driver's seat.

The car is not running yet the windows are fogged. She tries not to look but she cannot unsee the man in the driver's seat fulfilling his own wishes. The car is rocking, but he's the only one inside.

Meet Rest Stop Jack.

7
Runners Are Dicks

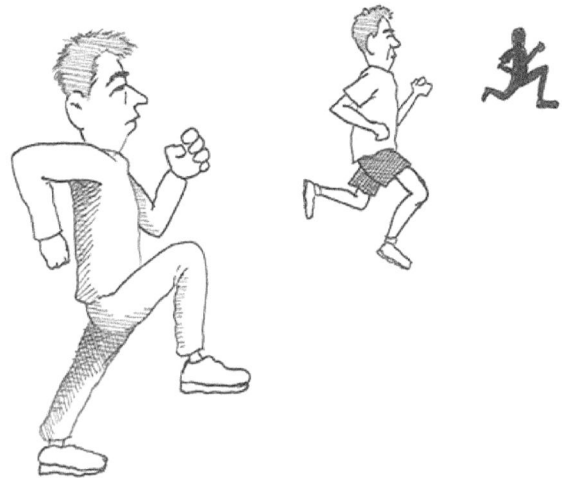

Another 5K race and I'm ready to go. The only reason I'm here is because I'm a reporter covering an event and take it upon myself to enter the race for a more in-depth report, which I do a couple times a year.

I run to feel good, about five miles - six or seven songs on the phone - enough to discover another backing vocal on another Stevie Wonder song, adding yet another gem of priceless data to my colossal collection of useless information.

At organized races, however, I feel out of place. The other runners share a common trait I haven't yet achieved: They're dicks.

Maybe they're normal and I'm a dick?

Today it begins in the parking lot behind Curtis Elementary School, which sits next to the Burnham Volunteer Fire Department and a big open field. You see them drive in and they have bike and kayak racks on their small, enviro-friendly cars with bumper stickers boasting of the podcasts, sports gear and 13.1 or 26.2 races they run.

They taunt you to judge them.

Walking in you overhear joking about how they hit a wall at twelve miles the other day or how their dog ate their $30 running socks. It's the kind of humor you hear on NPR shows – whiter than freshly fallen snow at a *Seinfeld* convention.

They have smiles on their faces but not happy smiles. It is a smile of 'yah I got this' or 'keep your eye on the ball' or 'one more day without meth.' To the younger runners it seems more a sentence of not-so-hard labor whereas the older runners treat it as a labor of love.

The Spandex-coated crowd is crawling with gear, all kinds of phones, armbands, heart monitors, watches, glasses, energy gels, compression clothing and ear buds. I wear Spandex shorts to prevent rashes, but I wear old shorts over them so I don't look like a dick.

I always wonder what music the over-40 crowd is listening to and usually surmise something like the Dave Matthews Band for the guys and Black-Eyed Peas for the ladies, whom I suspect are secretly proud there was a white girl in the band.

Among younger runners you find lots of Joshes, Justins and Jacobs along with Chloes, Crystals and Caitlyns. Their names are not so much a product of generation but of trendy parents who were (or still are) dicks.

The starting line, right before the race, is the grand march of the dicks. You see them running in place, stretching, hyperventilating or having Zen moments; all things that should have been (and probably were) done before the race.

It is nervous posing, usually by runners trying to impress their co-workers or their families, who cannot wait for this effin' race to end and go back home to sleep. These dicks usually hit a wall the second mile of a three-mile race.

The master of ceremonies on the PA is wild and zany and jumps on any opportunity for Monty Python or *Star Trek* references, which go clear over all heads at a 5K race. When it's seven in the morning and barely light, he keeps cutting in on the Bruno Mars and Maroon 5 songs to show how close he came to being a DJ (or how long it's been since he was).

"Are you guys ready to run!" he screams with the mic rubbing against his tonsils. Or, "Heeeyyy, okay!!! Where would you rather be at seven in the morning on Thanksgiving? Heh, heh heh."

The sound is always too loud and sure enough, Geraldine from the local savings bank must take the mic when he's done and give the runners an awkward thumbs up and "On your marks!"

The race begins.

Elderly runners are dicks too, and you notice a certain segment of them right away.

The closest-to-death line up at the front for photo ops and run so slow they nearly get trampled because everyone must immediately pass them.

This can be fun because it infuriates younger dicks. You know they want to say something vile but because they went to a private school or they're still in rehab, they smother their rage.

I too would like to alert the elders of their transgressions, but I have to wait in line. Instead, I use them to set a pick for me as I find a hole then hug the sideline for the next half mile and leave a hundred dicks in my wake.

It's moments like these I wonder why I didn't just do my usual run today. It's easy, free, close to home and I'm not surrounded by a running dick army (no offense to the former Texas congressman).

Just as I complete that thought I hear a voice from behind.

"Run faster or get out of the way!"

I turn to my left prepared for war when to my surprise I see my old friend Sam Thompson. He is in his 70s and has been running races since Nixon was president and looks like Bobby Darin if he lived and started running. He has an ear-to-ear grin and starts laughing when I recognize him.

"Nice move up the sideline. You look like Deion Sanders," he shouts.

"You look like Colonel Sanders," I respond.

And then it dawns on me. Sam is not a dick.

"Last race you said you were never coming back?" he yells, with wisdom that reflects his years as a school guidance counselor.

"I know," I say, huffing and puffing. "These runners get on my nerves."

"They're just here to have fun like you are," he replies with another grin. "Don't let it get to you. They're nervous. Everybody's afraid to disappoint themselves."

Then we hear a loud "On your left!!!" We both turn and it's three men in their 20s in matching yellow track suits, checking their watches and grunting what sound like words of encouragement to each other. They pass us like we're standing still, bumping other runners along the way.

"They look to be elite runners," I say, showing Sam I take his wise words to heart.

"They look to be elite dicks," he shouts back.

Suddenly I feel a bit better about myself with Sam's reassuring comment. I smile and wish him good luck.

"See you after the race."

He smiles back and offers one last bit of advice.

"Don't be a dick!"

Bob Deakin

8
Don't Go Near the Water

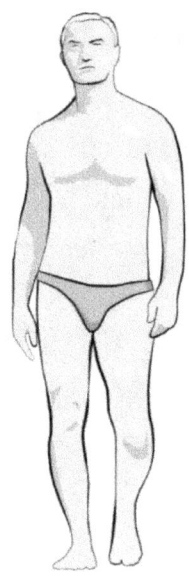

Here he comes,

Walking down the beach.

He gets the funniest looks from,

Everyone he meets.

No, no, he is not one of the Monkees, he's a grown man wearing a speedo. He's Mr. Skinny Mini, and he's a comin' this way.

"Honey hide the kids!" I hear the father of a family near me call to his wife, spotting the approaching man in the creepy-small speedo. "Skinny mini at nine o'clock."

Honey diverts the kids' attention as he rifles through a sack of beach toys for an object that doesn't exist just to divert his own attention.

Mr. Skinny Mini pays no mind. He doesn't see the family scurrying. He doesn't hear the people laughing. He has only one thing on his mind: Mr. Skinny Mini and the flock of women that surely must be gushing over him and his dangling sack of toys.

He's about 65 with slicked back, garishly colored black hair and something oily smeared all over his body, including his head.

He saunters along the water's edge like he's making a red-carpet entrance at the Oscars with a knowing smirk on his face.

In a modern-day version of *The Emperor's New Clothes*, Mr. Skinny Mini doesn't see a disturbingly small bathing suit, he sees the most stunningly beautiful bathing suit in the land, but the 'common people' on the beach see almost nothing at all. Either they are unfit or just too unsophisticated to revel in the beauty bestowed upon them.

Regardless, it's not the clothing that makes the man, it's what's on the inside that counts, and everyone on the beach has no choice but to count: Two; as in the number of potatoes fighting their way out of his bikini bottom, making everyone on the beach wish they were as far away as Idaho and pray that a pretty girl doesn't walk by, making something the shape of Florida enter the fray in the battle to escape his britches.

It is an instant theater of the awkward. Otherwise happy, comfortable people scramble to look away, walk in other directions, draw attention to something else or strike up conversations about anything but Mr. Skinny Mini and his wares.

The prettiest girls cringe, the toughest guys recoil and rambunctious children sit quietly by their parents. Even smoke from a distant fire drifts in another direction.

And just when it looks safe to head back into the water, it's time for the encore: His bum. Resembling two chihuahuas trapped in a balloon, Mr. Skinny Mini does his best to make sure anyone who misses the approaching train will surely marvel at the caboose.

He makes just as grand an exit as he did the entrance, living by the old showbiz adage, 'leave them wanting more.' Those on the beach simply wish he would leave.

Mr. Skinny Mini is just trying to be friendly, and he's too busy swinging to put anybody down. He is here to impress, and he's pulled out all the stops to make it happen. The living embodiment of one man's junk is another man's treasure.

Just like the emperor, beauty is in the eye of the beholder, not in the eyes of those obligated to do so, at least on a public beach. Whether it's a sack of toys, a couple of potatoes, the state of Florida or trapped chihuahuas, Mr. Skinny Mini has delivered a package no one wants to sign for.

9
Soccer Whore

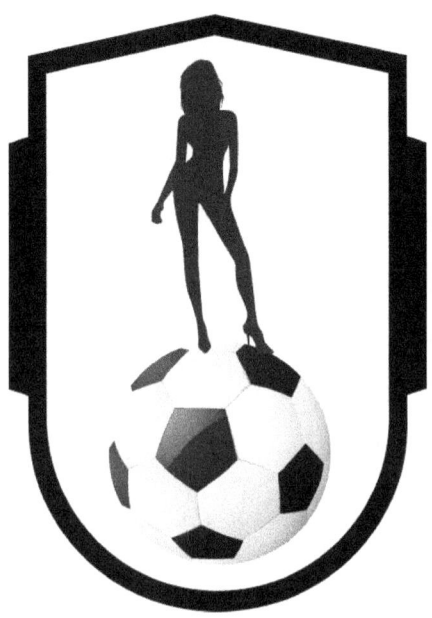

"She looks just like Patty Sherwood," Luke says to his wife, Liz, on this glorious sunny Saturday afternoon at their six-year-old son's soccer game at the Burnham Town Park.

They are looking at the 30-ish blond in the tight black sweats who keeps hopping out of her folding chair to make conversation with whomever is willing.

"Patty lived down the street from us on Raspberry Hill," Luke continues. "She's Billy Sherwood's little sister; nicest family you could imagine. When she grew up, she looked just like her," he added, nodding at the nameless blond.

"Did she have big boobs too?" Liz asks rhetorically, straight faced.

"Yep. Just like those," Luke retorts. "Almost like it was a strain on her back but not enough to require medical attention as far as we knew."

The focus of the couple's attention is apparently the mother of one of the children, though no one knows which one. She is also evidently single and none too shy about turning on her high beams in a well-lit area.

She approaches one guy sitting on a soccer ball and asks if he has any bug spray, joking that she has bite marks the size of half dollars on her neck, which immediately focuses his attention on her chest.

To another, she asks if he's going to need help getting up from his awkward position lying on a blanket in the grass, noting that she, too, is prone to finding herself sprawled out in compromising positions.

"Doesn't she know or care that everybody sees she's hitting on all these guys?" Liz thinks aloud, slowly turning her head toward the flirty soccer mom in amazement. "I mean, she's kind of pretty but please, the dark roots, slept-on hair, and can she lay off the cokes and chips for a little while?"

"The yoga pants are losing the battle with her ass, I give you that," Luke replies, "but put on a dress, turn down the lights, turn up the music, get the hair bouncin' and behavin' and different story," he assures. "A few beers and most guys are hittin' that."

The frisky soccer mom continues her act along the sidelines and at one point leaps out of her chair to retrieve the cell phone dropped by one of the soccer dads, putting it in his shirt pocket and patting it oh-so-gently for mock security, drawing the ire of his soccer wife.

Later, when she gets up to shout to the kids on the field - which she's been doing all day in a loud, piercing voice - one of the moms coldly asks her to stop standing in front of her family. The yoga-panted blonde answers with an angry glare then moves down a few steps and pats the butts of a young couple she knows well asking, "who's the bitch?"

They smile and she makes her way back to her chair, sits down and pops a Xanax.

"She is a sassy lassie aye?" Luke quips in his best brogue.

"She's a whore," Liz deadpans, slowly turning to him, daring him to reply, which he does.

"Just like Patty Sherwood."

10
Creep Filter

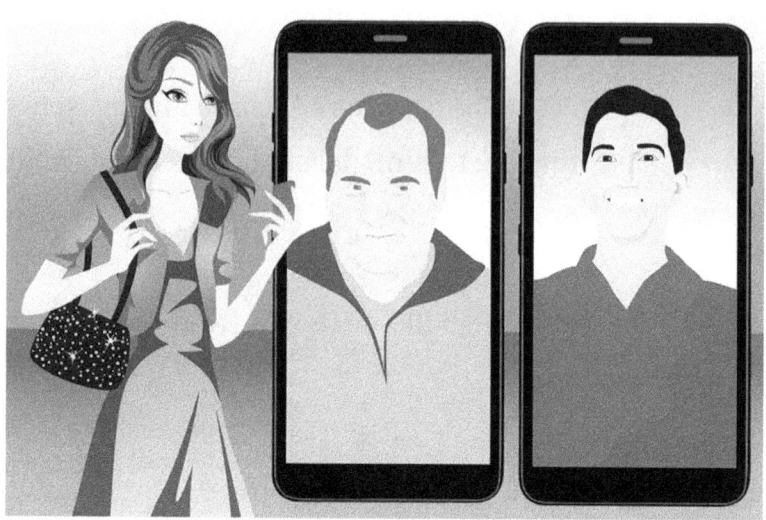

Alexis has had enough.

She has met another creep online who has laid down an Academy Award winning performance for a week until she discovers the character he truly is.

Yet another in a long line of bad auditions.

Alexis is a good friend and I keep telling her she doesn't need to play the online dating game. She's adorable and they're jerks. Or so it appears. She has a good job, lives in a nice small home near her sister in Burnham and lives a clean life. She has a young son too, which means she doesn't have the time or the tolerance for phonies, posers and criminals.

Is she a bad judge of character or are they good actors?

She doesn't want to be a judge. She just wants to enjoy life and share it with someone but needs a better way to pick through the weeds to get to the flowers.

Bring on CreepFilter.com, the dating site with a twist: instead of users writing their own profiles, a sophisticated analytical software writes it for them. They enter their social security number and a few personal details and a proprietary algorithm processes that with social networking, background and credit checks, health history and other exclusive insight creating a profile based on facts.

Here is an example of a Tinder profile submitted by Josh Silver of Greenwich, Connecticut:

X-Treme athlete, 26-years-old, 6-2, 190 with killer tan and exec position for Fortune 500. Sick into Kanye and love ladies into fitness, long hair and tatts. Seeking fulfilling connections with women who know their minds, speak the truth and dare to dream. Let's make some fireworks!

Here is what his profile looks like on CreepFilter.com:

31-year-old Jedidiah Silverio of Stratford, CT is seeking any woman who will respond to his profile. He's 6' 220 and works out on a stationary bike twice a week. Potential red flag is an obsession with dynamite. He has never been charged with a crime of demolition but has his eye on an old camper in the woods behind his apartment.

Kanye West fans beware: He loves to be seen listening to Kanye but cannot stand his beats. He is way into Michael Bublé. He does have a tan and works at a Wells Fargo call center and seeks women who like themselves. He genuinely hopes to find a nice girl but - to borrow from one of his Facebook posts - "I just haven't met you yet."

"Ugh! Are you serious!" Alexis grunts as we sit on the back of her truck parked along Town Line Road, talking relationships as she peruses profile after profile.

Just for kicks, she pulls one up from a female. Heidi from Stonesbury boasts of killing it in the car business on her Bumble account:

Confident, ripped sales closer, 28, looking for super-fit, clean cut confident winner. No lazy assess and no excuses. If you're with me it's 110-percent positive energy. Douche beards need not apply.

CreepFilter.com provides a little more info:

Heidi, 34, works part-time at a car dealership and teaches a Zumba class several times a year. She has been living with the same 54-year-old boyfriend for three years, does not like his two college-age daughters and the feeling is mutual.

She frequents the same downtown clubs every weekend and likes a good drink with her usual mix of Ambien and Ex. She is $25,000 in credit card debt and keeps reminding friends of her pending entrance into law school once she finishes her four-year degree, three years from now.

Alexis spots another profile.

37-year-old Jake Reilly is more into the visual on his Hinge.com profile. His photo flashes a thick swoosh of dark hair carefully blown forward with ample product, a solid build, tight graphic tee and dark tan with an overall look that belies his heritage and age.

Ladies... Let's cut to the chase. I complete you. I may look like The Rock but I'm a teddy bear. I don't play games... I play for keeps. Look for me in your dreams.

CreepFilter.com profile:

44-year-old John O'Reilly has three domestic dispute charges against him and sees himself as an identical twin to several movie stars. He is lifelong friends with a convicted anabolic steroid dealer, bartends on a cruise ship and is known as "Bro-Yo" for his frequent use of both terms and fancies himself selective with the ladies.

Based on previous profiles he seeks only women over 18, younger than 70, larger than a fox and smaller than a cow.

"Come on, Alexis, you're better than this," I say to her. "Okay, this new site gives you a more honest look at these guys, but you still have no idea."

She's stressed, and I bet she makes another hasty decision on her next selection in the dating game. She has poured over countless CreepFilter.com profiles but has yet to pick any flowers.

"You know," she responds with a sigh. "Maybe Tinder's not that bad. This is a little boring."

11
Hispanic Meghan

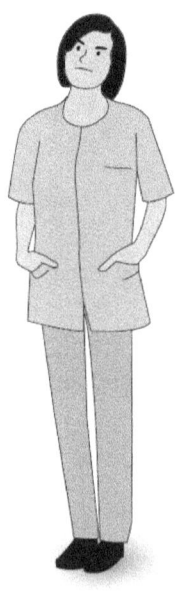

Aw snap! She looks just like my old friend, Meghan O'Malley from Burnham, only Hispanic.

I'm at a dentist's office in Arizona for a broken tooth while on vacation and do a double take at the hygienist who is tending to me today. Though my random thoughts are typically senseless, this one seems to make sense in an odd way. She looks like a Hispanic Meghan.

I don't expect it, I'm not ready for it and I can't ignore it, but I kind of like it because it feels like home.

Both are chica bonitas on the petite side with medium-length, flowing hair, piercing dark eyes and particularly distinctive eyebrows - which is the most striking similarity.

I am a long way from home and familiar faces are hard to come by, and the real Meghan is a dear friend and a lot of fun, so this is a good thing. She is one of those cats who is just easy to hang around with. Easy like Sunday mornin'.

Okay this is a medical visit, but she still looks like Meghan. Do I tell her? Of course not. It doesn't even matter. I keep a lid on it.

What is her name? This I can ask but I want to mull it over for a few. English names of Celtic origin are an unlikely translation to Spanish so certainly it is not Meghan, that would be culturally impossible and truly ironic. Now if it is Margarita and they call her 'Meg' for short, that would be an oddly poetic coincidence.

Not happening.

I wonder if she is anything like Meghan. Does she have the same sense of humor?
American Meghan does a mean Southern Belle accent. Who knows, maybe Hispanic Meghan does a dead-on accent of her own.

What does Hispanic Meghan stand for? I don't know – what does the real Meghan stand for? Who knows? What do I stand for? Anything? I'm overthinking this.

Alright. I spoil the fun and ask her name.

"Susana," she responds, reluctantly.

Beautiful name and I want to tell her she looks like my friend but we're strangers and I'm sure she doesn't care. Meghan might care but she might tell me to buzz off too, because she's like that, but she would do it in a nice way. I'm not sure about Susana. She is no-fooling-around serious.

Now I've got to know where She's from. It ain't Vermont.

"I am from Mexico," she replies to my bold inquiry, condescendingly.

"I hear they have fantastic beaches there," is all I have to offer.

"Please remain quiet and motionless so we can get an accurate x-ray," Susana quickly responds in a heavy accent, clearly annoyed.

I ponder taking a photo, but I think I've ticked her off enough and don't want to obsess over such a ridiculously random observation. Still, it is perplexing how Hispanic Meghan and American Meghan look like twin sisters despite such starkly opposite ethnicities.

Susana looks like she would be at home strolling along Puerto Vallarta with a glass of sangria while Meghan looks like she would be just as comfortable skipping along the Cliffs of Moher with a pint of Guinness.

Just then Susana completes the exam, removes the x-ray apron, gathers her things and curtly says someone will be in soon to take me to a different room.

"Excuse me," I say to her as she prepares to leave, "I just have to tell you. You look exactly like a good friend of mine."

"The doctor will be here soon," she responds without batting an eye.

She's kind of a bitch, I say to myself.

She leaves and closes the door when I hear her give instructions to the dental assistant on the other side, who is about to take over. Susana adds one final comment before walking away.

"He is - how you say - Douche bag?"

12
What's with the Long Ass?

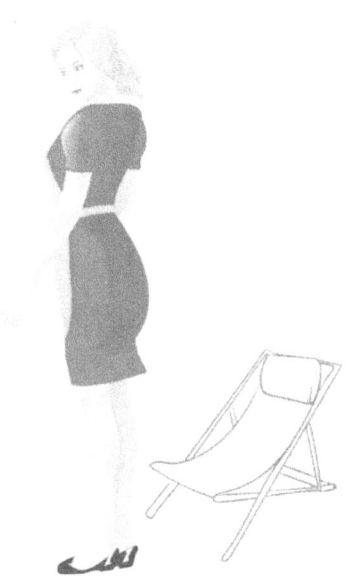

I have heard of big asses, fat asses, tight asses and lard asses, but I've never known anyone to have a long ass.

Not the case anymore.

Bob Deakin

I saw a woman at a crowded Burnham town meeting tonight who has such an appendage. She introduced herself as Elizabeth and is a pretty woman in her late 60s, not overweight and not unusually tall but she has an unusually long ass. It's hard to describe, just that it extends from the bottom of her back to the top of her legs to a length of nearly two feet.

I couldn't tell anything was amiss at first, when she was seated, but then she stood to speak to the room and holy cannoli, there it was. She didn't look like she'd been the victim of an accident or surgery gone wrong. It was as properly proportioned as it should be, I guess, not that I'd seen one like that before, but it was just so damn long.

How can that happen? Has she spent an inordinate amount of time sitting down through the course of her life? Perhaps she's done a lot of go-karting or row-boating? Maybe she went overseas on a religious retreat in the 70s and spent too much time sitting Indian style?

Speaking of overseas, she has a British accent which, strangely enough, makes the long ass make more sense. How, I'm not sure, but the elegant pronunciations and broader vowels compliment the drawn-out points she made at the meeting, which, in a roundabout way, all seem to match her figure.

I easily imagine she must have made the scene at many a high tea in England and scoffed down her share of crumpets and scones.

I also suspect she was a stranger to the soccer, or football field, in jolly old England, but that she'd probably been on a horse or two. Come to think of it, maybe she'd been a horse in a past life or closely related to one. Her ass was like that of a horse without the bulging muscles. She didn't have a horse face by any means, and I wouldn't ask her "what's with the long face" but I might ask her "what's with the long ass?"

Perhaps "A wee bit long in the bum wouldn't ya' say, m'lady?" would be more appropriate? She wouldn't like that, and I wouldn't ask her because I would't want her to kick my bum in front of everyone at the meeting.

I think I've answered my own question.

I wonder if she spends more money on seat cushions and undergarments over the course of a lifetime? Stands to reason. And where does she shop? The Big & Long section? Does she wear underwear? I certainly hope so, but she doesn't wear panties.

Nothing that covers that rig ends with "ies."

Why am I thinking about this right now?

I'm a newspaper reporter covering a town meeting on a Friday night, that's why.

I thought I was so much better than this?

Okay. Back to the meeting. Pay attention.

Elizabeth seems like a genuinely nice woman and very intuitive too. After all, she brought up good points at the meeting, which was organized to address the disproportionate, uncontrolled growth in her pretty little town.

The irony of it all.

13
I Met This Amazing Writer

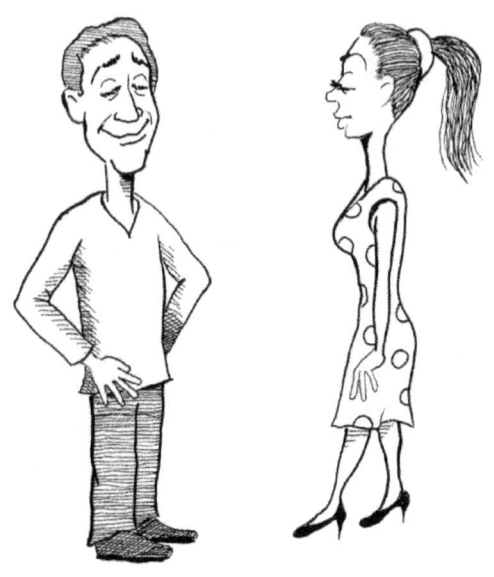

"I met this amazing writer the other night," says Ava to her friend, Jasmine. They are both college seniors home from break, sitting in the grass next to the baseball field enjoying a glass of wine.

"He is the most interesting guy," she continues excitedly, gazing toward the sun with a smile. "His name is Bradford. He was at Christian's party."

"What's so amazing about him?" Jasmine probes.

"You know how some people, like, just get it?" Ava asks. "I mean, he has no masquerade. He could talk Shakespeare or hip hop… Perspective like nobody."

"He *knows*." Jasmine surmises.

"Exactly!" Ava shouts. "He's so quick with a line but subtle. Good energy. I can't wait to read his stuff."

"What does he write?"

"Scriptwriter. He's done movies and commercials, I think."

"How do they do it?" Jasmine wonders aloud. "I mean, day after day, line after line. That's discipline."

"And he's got this Zen thing about him. He must be forty or seventy or something but he's just, you know, so dialed in to himself," Ava explains.

"What's he doing in Burnham?"

"He's working on a script for Tia Varrow," Ava says, referring to the renowned actress who lives in town.

"Wow! That explains it," Jasmine exclaims. "She's so beautiful. Wasn't she married to Joe DiMaggio?"

"No, it was Robert Goulet," Ava answers.

"Is he the one that sang "The Candy Man?"

"Yeah, that's the guy."

"You know everything," Jasmine flatters her friend, raising a toast.

"I read a lot of blogs. What can I say?" as they clink glasses.

"Are you gonna see Bradford again?" Jasmine presses.

"Yes! Friday. Sandy and Ned Bennett are having people over for burgers and beers. You have to come with me!"

Friday night arrives and the two beauties make an impressive entrance at the Bennett household. They know many of the guests, make themselves comfortable and make the rounds.

Before long Jasmine finds herself in conversation with Bradford. Ava's buildup has her a bit intimidated, but as an aspiring newscaster she's interested in his writing gig.

"How do you decide what projects to take on?" she asks.

"I think of it like traffic," he explains with an intense stare. "I see stop signs, green lights, construction, congestion and I make the best decision for that moment in time."

"So, you saw a green light on the project with Tia?" she surmises.

"Green lights all the way."

"What would be a red light?"

"Doing it for the money... If I didn't like the concept or the director that would be a yellow light."

"What if you liked the director and the concept but the producer had crazy political beliefs?"

"That would be a blinking yellow turn arrow."

Jasmine's heard the same analogies posed by celebrities. She's wise to him and senses Bradford's reaching to come off as profound.

"What if you're on a bus?" she answers back to throw him off.

"Then get off the bus."

"What's the hardest part of your job?" she continues, losing patience with his pompous demeanor.

"Looking like a writer," he tersely responds, crossing his arms, removing his glasses and resting them against his chin.

"Really? You don't look like that *good* of a writer," she says with a shrug, waiting a beat, which turns into a few beats.

Bradford breaks his gaze at her and hints at a smile. "What does a good writer look like?"

"You don't have a beard," she says, playing along. "What good writer doesn't have a beard?"

"I didn't green light the beard."

"I'm going to get off at this exit," she says, with a sarcastic sneer, and walks away.

A short while later Ava catches up with Bradford and they ease into a long discussion.

"How do you get asked to write a script for Tia Varrow?" Ava asks, flirtatiously tapping Bradford on the chest.

"She wanted a good script," he responds with a piercing glare. "My agent lives in Burnham too," he adds with a chuckle. "Location, location, location."

They inch a little closer as they talk and at one point, she changes the music to 80s rock, hoping to impress him with songs from his younger days. She waits until "I Can't Fight This Feeling Anymore" by REO Speedwagon plays before sidling up close to him, hoping for a tender moment.

"I know this song's kind of corny, but I have to admit I love it," she says with an embarrassed grin.

"Me too but I'm ashamed to tell anybody," he admits. "I always heard it was originally intended for The Village People."

"The Village People?" she asks with a confused grimace.

"Yah, but they turned it down. They thought it was too explicitly flamboyant. They didn't want to give their fans the right idea."

Ava is insulted but hasn't realized it yet. Her mood is thrown off as she walks away, starting to boil.

She reaches Jasmine.

"We were having this nice conversation," she exclaims, stuttering. "Then... he makes this stupid remark. I think he a jerk."

"You know what I think?" Jasmine declares. "He thinks he's smarter than everybody. HE'S A TOTAL ASSHOLE!"

14
Covid Chic

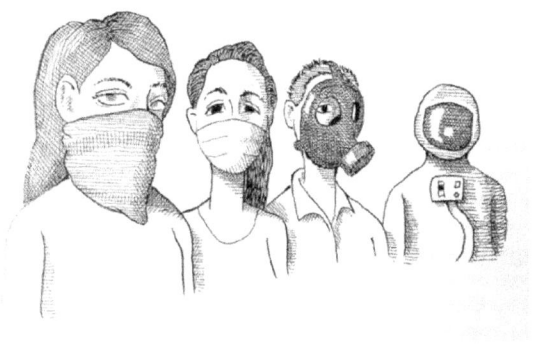

The Burnham Public Works Department took a few moments out of their schedule for occupational safety training Tuesday morning. According to Burnham Mayor Phil Stewart, the session was hastily scheduled on advice from the town attorney after several citizens complained that members of the public works department have been seen in Town Hall without a safety mask.

The presentation was focused on Covid-19 safety training and hosted by Rachael Fairlane, from nearby Kent, Connecticut, a compliance assistance specialist from the health department.

"My name's Rachael. I wear a mask!" the no-nonsense representative announces to the crew of six, sitting on folding chairs or leaning against trucks in the town garage.

"The town received several complaints on its Facebook page that certain members of the town crew have been spotted in Town Hall without a mask on," she announces at the outset of the meeting.

"Well, it's nice to be noticed," answers Town Foreman Ryan Kennedy, sarcastically, without missing a beat. "I'm always very concerned about what people say on Facebook."

"It has been a challenging time, I know," Rachael continues with a knowing nod.

"Normal is a thing of the past, like dry towns, tractor parades and marijuana dealers."

She grabs a box and places it on the table for all to see.

"What is now normal is a mask over the face and six feet of space, and that's why I'm here," she says in a sing-song voice. "Masks must be worn in all public places."

"Define public place," appeals crew member Artie Wells. Though he looks the part of a hit man, Artie plays the intellectual.

"I know it's a hassle, but you have to comply," Rachael interjects. "Not everyone's as big and healthy as you guys."

She reaches into the box and removes different models of face masks, replacing the light blue surgical mask she wears with a new

"ViroMask" featuring breathing valves on the side.

"Since we must protect ourselves anyway, we might as well be stylish about it," she says with her eyes showing a smile. "Just because we have to hide our faces doesn't mean we have to hide our expressions. Think of it like Halloween every day of the year."

Dirt, the crewmember who never says a word, steps away from the truck for a closer look.

"The town will purchase whatever type of mask you want but you have to settle on one design for all," Rachael continues. "I brought samples with me so here goes. I'll explain as we pass them around."

They smile reserved smiles as they handle the curious mix of choices.

"Many are going with the welder mask style with the clear shield covering the whole face. It looks effective but may be cumbersome for you guys. I get the feeling the wearer is preparing for a pie in the face at a fundraiser but that's just me."

Dirt puts it on and looks around.

"I don't like it. I can still see his face," Ryan deadpans, trying to get a reaction from Dirt.

"This bandana mask has a more urban feel," she demonstrates, holding it over her face. "One piece to wrap around your head and that's it. The material is thin enough to sift flour but who cares? You look like a biker or a gangster and it's good enough for government use.

"Another stylish option is the full-face respirator mask with single or dual cartridges. These are safe for any application, including painting and pressure washing. They weight a little more and the cartridges require replacement, but you look like a fly; not that there's anything wrong with that."

"Can we wear it while we're driving the truck?" asks Pauli, the new guy on the crew. The other men turn toward him with raised brows.

"Now why the hell would we need it while we're driving?" asks Craig. "I didn't know we drive school buses?"

"It's because Ryan smokes all day," Pauli retorts.

"Plastic, conforming face masks like this one have become a fashion statement," Rachael continues. "One has a plastic guard over the mouth with a fabric frame while the other is a one-piece, clear plastic mask that conforms to the face. They both are effective, just a matter of whether you're a fan of *Silence of the Lambs* or *Friday the 13th*."

"Why don't we just wear space suits around town?" Craig complains.

"Is there such a thing as a fashionable hazmat suit?" Artie inquires.

"Turns out there is," Rachael replies, ready with a rapid-fire pitch. "Low-end models go for less than a hundred and go up from there depending on the severity of the hazard. Simple to clean, easy on/off. Great vehicle for advertising. I'll take a Harry Potter model, thank you."

"How come so many people are always coughing in public places and nobody complains about that on Facebook?" Ryan asks as the crew straightens up, sudden interested in the conversation. "Am I missing something? Does everyone work in mines except me? Am I being rude for not coughing?"

"That always pisses me off too!" Craig fires back.

"Now everybody's getting vaccines anyway," Artie reasons. "Do we really need to be having this conversation?"

Rachael begins to lose her spark as she re-emphasizes the importance of protection on the job. She takes a deep breath, re-adjusts her posture and offers a different take on the situation for the guys when they're off the clock.

"If you're steadfast in your refusal to protect against the virus, or don't want to acknowledge it, you have an ace in the hole: Dollar stores."

The guys glance at each other.

"If you shop at dollar stores you are not even required to wear a mask," she poses, hands clasped, leaning toward the men. "They *want* to share viruses with you. Apparently, the logic is that their customers lives are worth about the same as their products, so why bother to clean or enforce safe practices."

"Higher profit margins, anyone?" Artie expounds.

"Stands to reason since there are three of them for every square mile," she answers pointing at him.

"Not in Burnham," Ryan quickly corrects her, getting grins from the crew.

"True but settle on one of these masks and wear it!" she urges as she packs up to leave. "I love it here. I'm from Kent. My brother is a member of the art group at the Brooks House in town and he loves it too."

"Yeah, well tell him to let us know what we can do better on Facebook," Ryan suggests with mock enthusiasm. "We'll be waiting with rapt attention."

15
The Six Degrees of Christmas

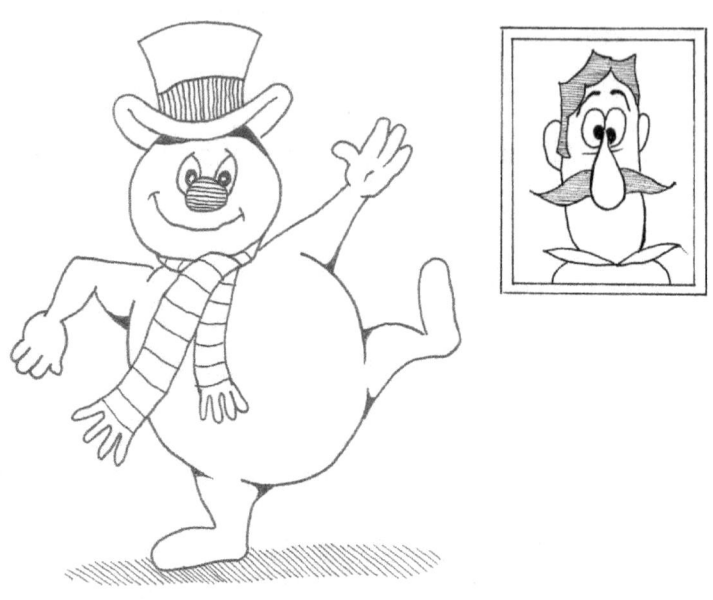

I love Christmas, especially the classic stop-motion, animated TV specials like *Rudolph the Red-Nosed Reindeer*, *Santa Claus is Coming to Town* and my favorite, the lesser-known *Year Without a Santa Claus*. I look forward to them almost as much as Christmas itself every year.

The Year Without a Santa Claus from 1974 was one of the final Christmas specials of its animated kind, and teased audiences that Santa was finally going to take a Christmas off. It features the voices of entertainers late in their careers and brings a bit more comedy to the show than previous specials.

Most exclusive to me, it always sets my mind off on a perpetual chain of thoughts. Here is how it goes:

Mrs. Claus is voiced by Shirley Booth, who I always confused with Shelly Winters. Shirley played the wise-cracking maid, Hazel, in the TV show of the same name while Shelly Winters was most noted in later years for her role in *The Poseidon Adventure.*

Also in *The Year Without a Santa Claus,* the Snow Miser was voiced by Dick Shawn, who played LSD (Lorenzo St. DuBois) in the original *The Producers* film in 1968. As the Snow Miser, he sang one half of the Snow Miser/Heat Miser ragtime-style showstoppers.

Yep. Same guy. Confounding that, I once thought Mr. Shawn and Max Baer Jr. - who played Jethro on *The Beverly Hillbillies* - were the same guy.

I remember the specials being sponsored by Jimmy Dean Sausage and I confused Mr. Dean with James Dean of *Rebel Without a Cause* fame. Jimmy Dean being a country singer, I went on to confuse him with Eddy Arnold because they were of a similar genre. That led to my blurring Eddy Arnold with Eddie Albert of *Green Acres* fame for obvious reasons.

Compounding this in the late 1970s, Eddie Albert starred as a detective in the TV crime drama, *Switch*, with Robert Wagner, who I constantly confused with Lyle Waggoner, a regular on *The Carol Burnett Show*. Mr. Waggoner looked like Robert

Wagner and the name similarity didn't help, especially since Robert Wagner was married to Natalie Wood, who I sometimes confused with Joanne Woodward, wife of Paul Newman, because of their wooden names.

This also reminds me of the 1973 version of the movie, *Miracle on 34th Street* starring Sebastian Cabot. The cast includes both David Doyle and Tom Bosley, whom I was forever mistaking for each other because of their physical resemblance. Tom Bosley was most noted as Richie Cunningham's father on the TV show, *Happy Days*. Adding to the interlocking ball of confusion was Doyle's most memorable role on *Charlie's Angels*. His character's name: John Bosley.

Perhaps the most bizarre cross-up involves actor Paul Benedict, who played the British neighbor, Mr. Bentley, on *The Jeffersons* TV show. When I was little and used to watch the *Frosty the Snowman* cartoon Christmas special featuring the evil

Professor Hinkle, who gives Frosty the magic hat, I thought that Paul Benedict and the animated Professor Hinkle were the same person, even though one was real and the other a cartoon.

They both had jutting chins, floppy hairstyles, looked middle-aged nerdy and spoke with similar voices and accents. Don't ask me how the mis-association happened but to this day, whenever I see Mr. Bentley on *The Jeffersons* or Professor Hinkle on *Frosty the Snowman*, I'm thinking of the other guy.

The Year Without a Santa Claus was produced by the team of Rankin/Bass, who created *Rudolph the Red-Nosed Reindeer* and *Santa Claus is Coming to Town*, but I always confused them with the team of Hanna-Barbera, who created *The Flintstones*, *Tom and Jerry* and *The Jetsons* cartoons.

Now that I think of it, Dick Shawn was also among the star-studded cast of *It's a Mad, Mad, Mad, Mad World*, which included, of all people, Mickey Rooney, who –

what do you know – voiced the role of Santa in *The Year Without a Santa Claus.*

We're all connected somehow. Especially at Christmas time.

16
Poets with Stupid Names I

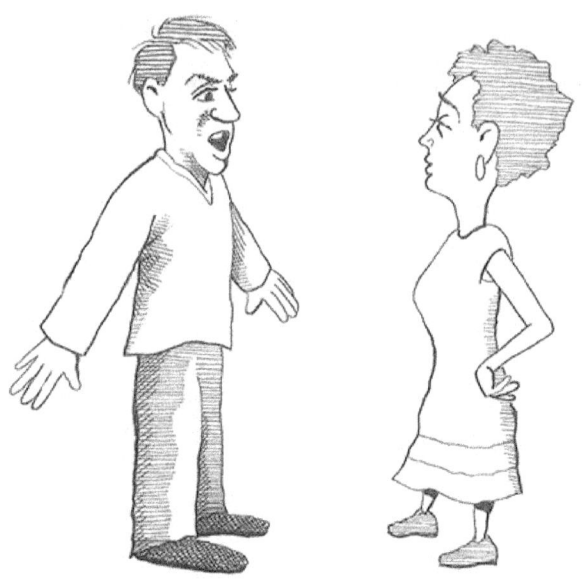

I am invited to a party the other day by a member of the poetry group I just joined and although skeptical at first, it turns out I meet a bunch of remarkably interesting people, many of whom have exotic names such as Felicity, Sterling, Vespa and November.

My name being Bob, I almost feel too common to be in their company but make the best of it and welcome the opportunity to expand my social circle beyond Burnham.

Everything is going great. We're discussing compelling topics, exchanging ideas and views of the world and I'm fitting in rather nicely. Rainn, the party hostess and leader of the Exposed Roots Poetry Troupe - of which many here are members - is quite the social butterfly with a habit of politely shouting the name of the person she converses or jokes with. Early in the party that is Sterling and Vespa.

After a while, however, the names start to get to me.

Why would someone name their daughter November, I ask myself as I look across the room? Nice name, but everyone who meets her must wonder if that's the month she was born. If not, there must be a sappy story behind it.

Just then, Tobias walks up and asks what I do for a living. I don't even ask him. He's Tobias, and that sounds like a full-time job.

Next up Felicity. I bump into her as we both walk into the kitchen to freshen our cocktails and she's quite the vixen. She's had a few already and asks me if I'm friends with Vespa. I think to myself that I had once ridden a Vespa when I was a kid but figure it's not appropriate to joke about her name just yet.

In the next hour I am introduced to El Delaney, who everyone refers to by her full name yet is obviously of Asian heritage with a thick accent. I then meet Sterling and his wife, Isis, then Alexandrianna and her wife, Sarah-Sandra, whose name I easily
remember because she looks like actress Sandy Duncan, who, oddly, I had not thought of in 25 years.

Didn't she play Peter Pan? I ask myself about Ms. Duncan, zoning out, distracted by all the names. "Or was she on *Room 222*?"

Finally, I am introduced to a woman named Topaz and her friend, Niles. I repeat out loud, "Topaz and Niles?" I then glance around as if this is a joke with all the exotic names.

"Your name is Topaz?" I ask, condescendingly, drawing uncomfortable stares from around the room. "Is that a nickname? Who started calling you that?"

Turns out it was her father who named her at birth, inspired by a family heirloom handed down to him by his grandmother, who emigrated from Europe during World War II.

She remains surprisingly calm despite my insult and explains that her father was a geologist and that the Topaz also held supreme significance to him because the Blue Topaz is her birthstone, from the month of December.

"Well, that's significant," I reason, uncomfortably, looking around for anyone to jump in and save me. I think to myself, *what would Oprah Winfrey do in this situation*, but nothing comes to me.

"Do you write poetry too?" I ask, nervously. "Felicity said a lot of people here are into poetry."

"As a matter of fact, I do," Topaz says in a standoffish manner. "Most of us know each other from disparate poetry meetups."

I get the feeling I am one remark away from being asked to leave. Just then, Felicity takes a few steps my way and collapses in my arms. Thank goodness she's a drunken mess, maybe even high on pills, but she's taken the attention away from me. I hold her up and gently carry her to the couch to lie her down.

"I know you, don't I?" she moans.

"Yeah, it's Bob," I remind her.

"That's a funny name," she mumbles, loud enough for everyone to hear.

"I know. At this party it's hilarious. I'm surprised they let me in here."

That remark sets off Topaz, who turns and shoots me with a look to kill.

"You're a jerk," she says to me, loudly and sternly, hands on hips. "Who invited you here?"

"I forget," I reply. "He had a really stupid name."

17
Poets with Stupid Names II

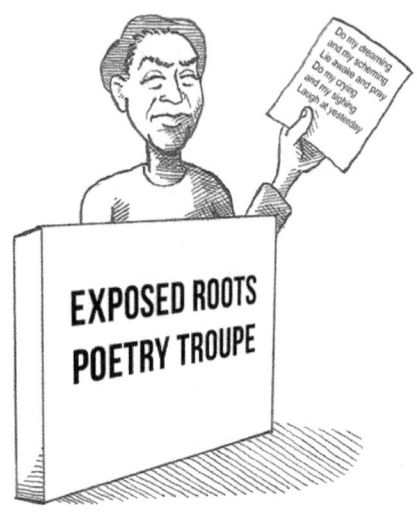

Checking my email this morning I cannot believe what I see. It's a message from Rainn of the Exposed Roots Poetry Troupe, inviting me to a 'poetry explosion' Wednesday night at the Hard Times Tavern. After the way I insulted her friend Topaz at the party last Friday, I figure Rainn would rather get struck by lightning than see me again.

This is a human-composed, live, personalized email too, mentioning my name and everything (I didn't think anyone sent those anymore). That is nice of her, but I must admit I have to roll my eyes at part of the inspirational message in the signature of her email: "Dance like no one's watching."

Come on Rainn... I sigh to myself. I like the sentiment, but I'm embarrassed for her including it in her email. Maybe I should include "Email like no one's reading" in a new inspirational message of my own.

I then catch myself, take a deep breath, toss aside my cynicism and realize once again that I must open the window of my soul and let the breeze of tolerance blow in. This is the new me, expanding my horizons.

Bob Deakin

Wednesday night arrives and I cannot believe I am here at the Hard Times, proud for having the courage to show up. Rainn is here. So is Tobias, November and - low and behold - Topaz.

Rainn walks over, gives me a big hug and a warm welcome. I ask what a poetry explosion is since I cannot find it in the dictionary, and she explains it as well as a poet can be expected to. I chat with her for a bit then tepidly make my way over to Topaz and, hat in hand, apologize for deriding her name at Friday night's party. She is unexpectedly gracious about it and welcomes me to sit with her and the others – all of whom were also at the party.

Tobias is too busy being Tobias to remember me and November is so high on organic good vibes that she is blinded by the enlightenment.

I struggle to make myself comfortable in the uncomfortable, 50-year-old wooden chair as the first reader of the evening finishes his poem. There is no outward applause, just positive vibes sent his way, so I raise my hands and snap my fingers repeatedly like I once saw in a beatnik movie from the 50s. Guess what? A couple in the corner does the same thing! I flash them the peace sign in response but suddenly that seems so 60s of me and I rein it back in.

Next up is a woman whom I recognize from the fiction writing group where I met Rainn and some of the others. I don't know her name, but I lean over to Rainn and ask, "Is that the nine-eleven lady?"

Rainn blushes and shyly says, "That's Sabine. Yes. She does often invoke September 11 in her poetry."

"I thought that was her. I love her work," I reply, lying through my teeth. "She's got a distinctly special touch."

I don't appreciate someone using 9/11 for self-serving purposes but I'd caused enough trouble at the previous gathering and cannot assume all of Sabine's poetry focuses on 9/11 so I just sit back, shut up and take it in.

Oh, the days dwindle down to a precious few,
  and so much more for those who never knew.
  Those on the ground - a sunny day of dread.
  In the air - I pray they knew not what lie ahead.

As I load my imaginary revolver, Sabine begins to cry and cannot continue reading. She steps back from the microphone and buries her face in her hands as several in the audience get up and help her offstage, James Brown style without the cape. I then internally channel her poetic meter:

Moved to tears by what she invokes,
  suffocated is she, by her own cloak:

The comedienne dies laughing at her own joke.

How fortuitous and ironic her breakdown is, I say to myself, looking down at the floor. Now I don't have to make a scene again like I did last Friday. One more word of verse and I might have gone John Wilkes Booth on Sabine, but I didn't. And no one knows any better. Now I'm just another writer among writers. Maybe even a poet among poets.

I look up and see Rainn rushing to console Sabine. Tobias and November are deep in conversation with themselves, and Topaz is expounding upon the origin of her name to a new arrival at the poetry explosion.

I almost fit in.

18
Frankie's Studio

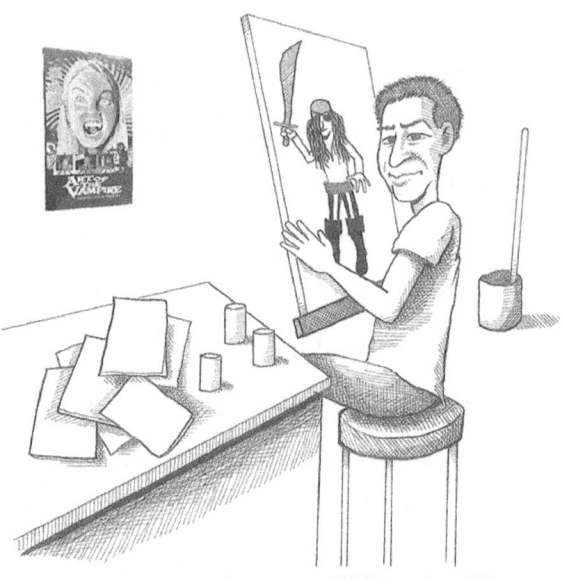

"Can't you knock first?" yells Frankie, the artist, angry and red-faced, lowering his palette to face the door. He is standing in a small, poorly lit room with worthless objects on the floor, sweating over an oil painting of a pirate on a cruise ship.

The room is scattered with everything from an ashtray and industrial adhesives to nude photos, bottles, mops and buckets. The workspace is crammed into a small piece of a large, elegant four square, colonial revival home near Town Hall. It is the former Brooks House and remains a regal landmark in the center of Burnham.

It is not the ideal artist's studio but the only one left in town for Frankie Cabrera. Over the years, he's used other public buildings, but changing times and property owners have left him in a one-room former storage closet.

They've also left him bitter and unfocused. This is a scheduled visit by students from the local high school to see his latest work in progress, but Frankie is not ready.

The genesis of the visit came at a reception at Burnham Free Library several weeks previous. The gala event celebrated an exhibit of surrealism in oil enamels by Frankie's friend. Hostess Twinkies were served along with copious amounts of Martini & Rossi Asti Spumante.

Frankie struck up a friendship with the bongo player at the event, who turned out to be Art Teacher Bo Digby from Curtis High School. After several refills of Spumante, Frankie overstated the expanse and splendor of his studio before inviting Mr. Digby to bring his students for an educational tour.

Fast forward to the day of the visit.

Mr. Digby apologizes as they file in and look at the painting and the room. He and the students are surprised at the meager and cluttered state of the room, and he has a brief but tense chat with Frankie before leading them out.

Frankie asks for a few minutes to tidy up then reluctantly agrees to come and speak to the group a few minutes later to offer insight into his current project.

The students make their way to the kitchen of the Brooks House and sit to discuss what they have just witnessed. As awkward as the situation is, energy is high, and they are bouncing in their seats to make comments. Mr. Digby is annoyed at Frankie's exaggeration of the studio but keeps a positive vibe.

"It was an unconventional display of inspiration, of course, but aren't they all," Mr. Digby begins. "Did anyone notice how important it was for the artist, right there during our tour, to re-position the bucket in such a carefully chosen location? A true artist is never satisfied with random placement of his subjects."

"It was amazing," interjects Tinka, a junior at Curtis, hands on her knees in glee. "That was such a compelling statement. I've never had a work of art hit me like that before. It was really surreal."

"I see a man of the sea in horrible pain," offers Miguel, a senior, frantically eager to explain Frankie's use of color, texture and found treasures. "His ability to emote an emotion is incomparably emotional."

Other students follow in praising the artist's work, complimenting everything from the pirate and the paintings on the wall to the mop in the bucket on the floor.

Twenty minutes later, Frankie finally arrives to speak and answer questions.

"What is the message you are trying to send with this compelling work?" Mr. Digby eloquently inquires, kicking off questioning.

"I must start by apologizing to you all," Frankie says, his face painted with shame. "I've been up for three days drinking beer, sniffing glue, looking at porn and trying to fix the damn leak in the ceiling."

19
Straw Hat Weirdo

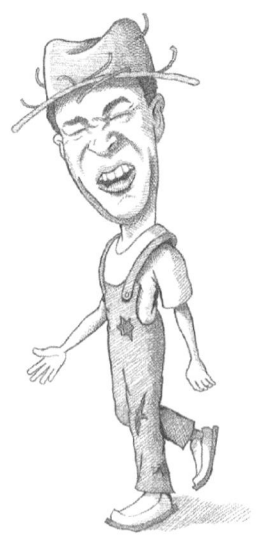

He's back again. The skinny guy with the straw hat, torn overalls and yellow, girly shoes. What a weirdo! Whenever he shows up, so does trouble.

His name is Dirt, but everyone knows him as the skinny guy with the straw hat, torn overalls and yellow, girly shoes. Something is always missing, broken or painted a funny color after he makes an appearance.

He works for the Burnham Public Works Department and one of his titles is steward for the Brooks House on Middle Street. He tends the yard and keeps the large, aristocratic home presentable; upstairs for tap-dancing classes and downstairs for artists, who use several small rooms and closets as studios.

Dirt is painfully antisocial and moves quietly wherever he goes, desperately seeking to avoid human interaction. As a result, he's rarely noticed but often suspected of malfeasance.

Last month, Frankie Cabrera, one of the artists, at home after a long night in the studio, realized only too late that he left his iPad in the kitchen of the Brooks House.

If somebody finds it, they'll hold it for me, he assured himself as he lay his head on the pillow for the night, comforted by the camaraderie of his fellow artists.

He returned in the morning only to find his iPad stomped to a thousand pieces on the kitchen floor.

"Who the hell did this!" he screamed, crushed with disappointment.

"It was a skinny guy with a straw hat, torn overalls and yellow, girly shoes," said Seth Fairlane, another artist, stepping into the kitchen to counsel him.

Seth explained that his Mannheim Steamroller vinyl LP collection went missing the previous week, never to be found. He suspected it was Dirt because that was his day to mow the lawn. "He comes here on Tuesdays. Real weirdo."

The following Tuesday, Lynn, another artist at the studio, completed a sculpture of The Burnham Free Library, cut from a single piece of teak wood. It was a commissioned work and took her nearly ten weeks to complete. It was the darling of the local art scene and upon completion placed on display in the foyer for all to see.

That afternoon, Keisha, upstairs after bidding farewell to her tap-dancing students at the end of the day, spied the security monitor and noticed activity on the first floor. In her report to police, she described a man swinging an ax at Lynn's sculpture, which was on fire. She credited her artist's intuition for knowing something wasn't right, and went downstairs to investigate.

By the time she got there, she said a man was skipping out the door. The sculpture was chopped in hundreds of pieces, all of them burning, and the heat and smoke set off the alarm, summoning the police and fire departments.

"He was very skinny, with a straw hat, torn overalls and yellow, girly shoes," Keisha recounted to Sergeant Jeff Casey of the Burnham Police.

"Did you notice anything strange about his behavior?" he asked.

"He was very weird," she said. "When I asked, he said he was here to fix the plumbing, but he wasn't dressed like a plumber, and it didn't look like a plumber's ax he was wielding."

"That is weird," Sergeant Casey responded before asking what a plumber's ax looks like.

After the incident, Keisha and Seth had a long, thoughtful and ultimately cozy conversation. They decided to contact Mayor Stewart about the issue and confront Dirt as soon as they could find him.

Nothing more came of it until this morning when Julie brought in a brand-new espresso machine for her fellow artists and proudly set it up on the kitchen counter. By noon it had been inexplicably ripped from the wall and tossed out the second-story window and splattered on the sidewalk.

Tears flooded down her cheeks after discovering the vile act as she carried the destroyed machine back into the house.

"Who! What! Why?" she cried, comforted by the artists, all staring at the carnage in disbelief.

"It was the skinny guy with the straw hat, torn overalls and yellow, girly shoes," Seth divulged as everyone stared at their feet in search of an answer. "Real weirdo!"

Just then rhythmic tapping and crashes come from upstairs.

"It was thrown from the second floor!" Lynn shouts.

"That's right!" Frankie yells back as they all look at each other and run to the stairs, tripping over each other. Upon reaching the second floor their eyes fly wide open as they gasp in horror.

It's Keisha, wildly tap-dancing on album covers, kicking espresso cups and throwing vinyl LPs all over the room like frisbees, exploding as they hit the walls. Seth's jaw drops as he sees it's his Mannheim Steamroller albums.

Tears well up as he is hit with the betrayal of a friend and the loss of his prized collection. The artists all look at each other, speechless.

Just then, Dirt shows up out of nowhere, rushes up the stairs in time to witness Keisha's hysterics.

"What a weirdo!" he screams in horror.

20
Afternoon Delight

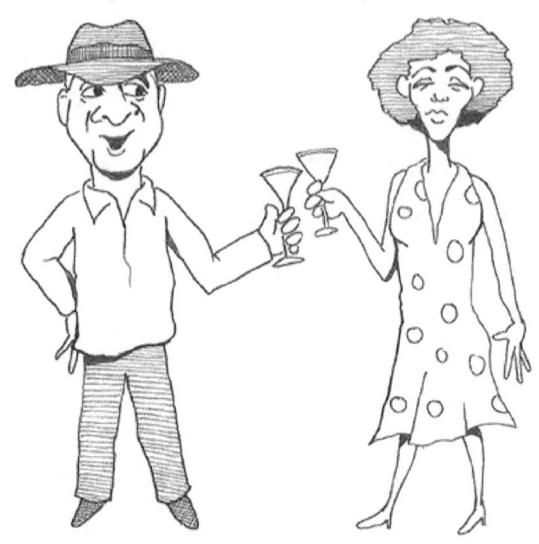

One of these days I'm going to find the estate sale from heaven. I've been chasing estate sales, tag sales, yard sales, garage sales, rummage sales, flea markets, swap meets and other people's stuff for years. My name is Antonio Zaccaro. I carry cash and drive a truck.

Some people call me aggressive. Some people call me obnoxious. Others call me a walking appraisal. I call myself Tony the Tagger. The ladies just call me.

If you see my truck back into your driveway, consider yourself lucky. If you don't sell that priceless armoire your grandmother left you, at least you'll know what it's worth; that is, if you're not too distracted by the friendship you just struck up with the charismatic man in the fedora.

My weekends are spent in the homes of others. You see all types at these events, and the online reseller generation hasn't stopped me yet. They can have their early mornings, bad parking and price haggling. I'll wait it out for the hidden gems.

Here's a description of my favorite sale of all time. It was six months ago and it was almost perfect.

I find a sale on a sunny Saturday afternoon that somehow fell off the grid of the professional taggers. I park in the large, shaded driveway, not on a narrow two-lane major thoroughfare, and I don't feel like I'm walking onto the set of *King of the Hill* if it wasn't a cartoon. I comfortably get out of my truck and no crowds are there to fight through, the hosts have social skills, the guests are friendly and the neighbor isn't operating a leaf blower.

I leisurely stroll into the home when a lovely female hostess arrives, leading me through the spotless, palatial estate. I take in the sights, observe the merchandise – all tagged with prices – and wring my hands at the countless prospects while the score of an Italian film from the 1960s plays softly in the background.

Right away I find an old Hammond B3 organ, just like the ones on the classic pop songs, and it works. I confirm the model, see all the parts are in place, and make it known to the hostess I plan to walk out with it, and find that she wants only $50, a significant discount from the tens of thousands of dollars I would expect to pay.

I then stroll to another room to find a vibraphone with the electric pickups and foot-controlled damper bar in place, also working, also with a price tag of $50, again a solid discount from the several thousand dollars I would expect. Once the purchase is secured and before I make my way across the room, I stumble over a Bang & Olufsen turntable, never used and still in the box from 1982. There is no price tag on it, but the hostess doesn't know what it is and tells me I can have it for, "does five dollars sound fair?"

Indeed, it does. I secure it and continue browsing.

I pass the countless antiques, Ansel Adams prints, 1920s cuckoo clocks, 1930s telephones, 1940s baseball memorabilia and 1950s neon Ballantine Ale signs from the taverns of Manhattan, all while making small talk with the hostess.

I then spot a dark blue, sharkskin suit with matching white handkerchief and cufflinks, circa 1962, a la Dean Martin in the Rat Pack movies. It's a perfect match for my size and the hostess modestly utters, "would you be interested in a cocktail mixer set, including etched-glass martini shaker, ice bucket, silver-plated snifters, bottle stopper and tan leather case from the same era?"

"Indeed, I would, although I only have so much to spend, and I would like the suit, so…"

All my dreams of the 60s are nearly complete and I take a complementary walk around, ponder a few more purchases, and notice that I'm a bit parched.

"Would you care for a Martini?" the hostess offers, introducing herself as Gabriela. "If you don't mind vintage glasses from the set of Hitchcock's *Dial M for Murder*, I'd be happy to pour you one."

"Well... Perhaps you could twist my arm," I politely respond with a warm smile.

Gabriela, who has what sounds to be an Italian accent and is the spitting image of Sophia Loren in 1960, pours two and hands me one, then gently caresses my hair with a swath of her hand, admitting she's a bit shy for being so forward on a Saturday at an estate sale.

"My sincerest thanks to you, my dear," I whisper, raising my glass toward hers. "Such a lovely day among such opulence, with such a charming hostess being so kind to a gentleman stranger. What, may I ask, have I done to deserve such delight?"

Just then, her phone rings.

"Please excuse me," she says, placing her hands in prayer position and tilting her head toward me. "I'm expecting a call from my father. He's not feeling well and I need to answer."

She steps away and picks up her phone underneath the stained-glass Tiffany lamp. She speaks just a few words before ending the call and returning, but she breaks a heel and crashes hard, taking the crystal decanter of Martinis with her.

"Gabriela!" I shout and lunge toward her.

We're both in shock at the violence of the fall but after a moment of kneeling on the floor beside her, both of us surrounded by broken glass, gin and vermouth, she doesn't appear to be seriously injured. Nonetheless, I help her up, clean the mess and make sure she's comfortable.

A few moments pass and it's apparent she is fine and just needs a rest and some time to herself. I gather my things and prepare to leave.

"Oh, just one more thing," I ask. "Is your father alright?"

"I don't know," she says with an air of confusion. "It was the oddest thing. A stranger was calling, telling me my automobile warranty has expired."

21
A-Hole in the Fedora

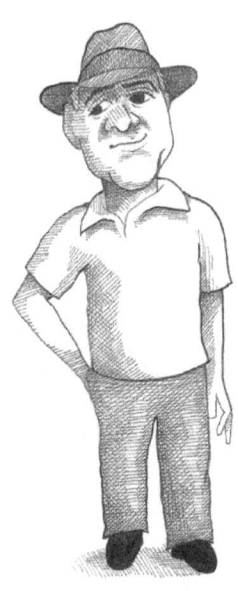

Tag sales are tedious events for homeowners but without the patrons, it does not work. Most tag sale shoppers make a stop a couple times a year, but some are professionals known for their years of dedication to the craft.

I was looking to write a profile on professional taggers, and asked around to find one such expert and was led to Antonio 'Tony the Tagger' Zaccaro of Burnham, CT. He earns his nickname by virtue of decades as a familiar face at tag sales and for being featured on both the *Good Morning America* and *Hoarders* TV shows.

I met him at a sale in Greenwich, courtesy of homeowner Shari Fishman, who has seen him at estate sales for years. Affable and youthful for a man of 68, Zaccaro comes off as a know-it-all talking about all things as he explains his strategy. He is game for the interview and I'm grateful for his time and generosity.

"First thing I do at every sale is back my truck up the driveway," he arrogantly exclaims. "Right away they start showing me around and prices drop like dollars at a strip club."

He attests even those that don't know him quickly spot the tall man in denim strolling confidently through the throngs of taggers with his trademark fedora tilted slightly to the left.

"You can't help but notice me," he assures with a wink. "Especially the ladies."

He has been attending sales throughout the Connecticut-Massachusetts-New York area since the 1970s and is known for his penchant for late 19th Century furniture, musical instruments and golden-age Hollywood memorabilia. He not only longs for artifacts, he says, but genuinely believes he is entitled to them.

Whether it is an oak cabinet Thomas Edison may have owned or a poster of Raquel Welch, Tony the Tagger is determined to call it his own.

"One of the most memorable sales I've been to was held by a legend of stage, screen and television," he regales, sauntering through the first home of the day, employing a dramatic pause and taunting me with his good fortune. He elaborates the tale of rubbing elbows with the star before divulging her name.

"Valerie Harper," he announces, slowly and deliberately, leaning forward for emphasis. He details the day spent at the star's home examining items for sale and subsequent cozy conversation he struck up with her.

"We spent the day together at her estate and ended up rubbing a little more than elbows," he continues with a knowing laugh.

It all began, he says, with a few innocent questions about a Victorian walnut spoon back chair, which led to a personal tour of her movie memorabilia collection and before he knew it, they locked eyes, both leaning over a vintage cocktail table when their hands touched for the first time.

"You can't put a price tag on what I walked away with that day," Zaccaro says, smiling, leaning back on an antique French sofa at the Fishman home, clasping his hands behind his head.

Asked if he was alleging to have slept with Ms. Harper – made famous by her role as next-door neighbor 'Rhoda' on *The Mary Tyler Moore Show* – Zaccaro asked, again with a wink, "Who said anything about sleeping?"

While Zaccaro is well-known among tag sale hosts, it does not equate to admiration. I managed to find one such host in Alecia Washington, owner of a palatial estate in Northampton, MA, worthy of Bruce Wayne and his ward.

"He's a jerk," she says, resolutely. "He walks in like he owns the place and makes low-ball offers on authentic hand-made pieces from the 1800s like they're cheap TVs. He's married and spends more time hitting on me and other clientele like he's at a strip club."

Told of the coincidental strip club analogy Zaccaro used earlier, she doesn't bite on an offer for further comment.

I also spoke to Maggie Bjornsen of Stonesbury, Connecticut.

"My next-door neighbor, Stephanie, hosts estate sales for New York homeowners every summer and this guy's been showing up for years," she confirmed, rolling her eyes. "He's so full of himself he even gave himself a nickname; 'Tony the Tagger.' Stephanie refers to him as the a-hole in the fedora."

Told of what the estate sale hosts said of him, Zaccaro doesn't blink, choosing instead to explain the difference between an authentic Universal Studios poster and a fake. Asked what motivates him to continue his week-to-week performance attending sales year after year he conceitedly repeats a quote by an old baseball star.

"There is always some kid who may be seeing me for the first or last time and I owe him my best."

Confronted with the fact that very few children go to tag sales and even fewer show up to see him, he downplays his role as a local celebrity.

"Ah, I'm just a simple man with simple tastes," he states, again with a wink and a grin. "Who can resist a 19th Century gem or an authentic framed *Casablanca* promo? I also can't help it if the ladies can't resist a tall, confident, handsome man in a fedora."

Perhaps they cannot, but when it comes time to get rid of an old relic, a warm body with a wallet often seems irresistible.

Ms. Bjornson was later asked if any of Stephanie's clients, by coincidence, were TV stars in the 70s and said no, then looked up, curiously.

"You know," she remembered, "everybody always tells Stephanie she looks just like the next-door neighbor on *The Mary Tyler Moore Show*.

22
Tip Your Bartender

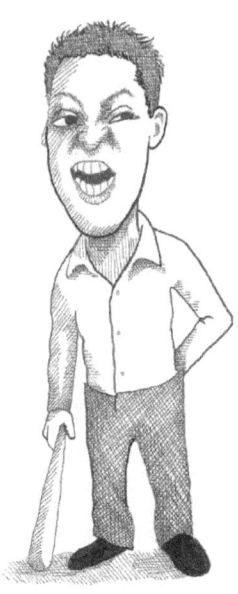

Police responded to a disturbance at the home of Ryan and Daphne Kennedy of Northrop Street in Burnham early Saturday morning when a traffic jam formed as dozens of people showed up for a much-anticipated tag sale.

"Six-thirty in the f***in' morning and there's twenty a**holes in my driveway ringing my f***in' doorbell," Mr. Kennedy grumbled to reporters later that morning as he removed balloons attached to his mailbox.

Kennedy – also the foreman of the Burnham Public Works Department – was initially startled by the commotion outside and when they refused to leave, he flew into a rage and returned with a baseball bat to scare them away, only to receive several offers for the bat.

Respondents produced an ad in the local newspaper showing a tag sale slated for 7 am at that address on that day, which police took into evidence.

Northrop Road resident, Stacey Gillen, speaking to a reporter shortly thereafter, said it's unlikely her neighbors would host a tag sale.

"He's so dang cheap he'd haggle every f***in' item," she said from her driveway, nursing a bloody mary in her robe and slippers. "And if Daphne go and start flappin' her gums they ain't gonna sell nothin.'"

Local teacher Michael Tuzman and his wife were two of the first on the scene at the Kennedy home at 6:30 am, ready for the start of their well-organized day. I spoke to him after the ruckus and found that expert taggers plan their day to the minute to snap up the best items before regular humans show up.

"We were following our itinerary through the south-central quadrant of Ritchfield County – based on the rising sun – before moving to southeast quadrant two at coordinate 41.5047028, - 73.3623780," Tuzman explained as I listened in amazement. "From here we move to central sectors one and two, then to the north and west, as is normal for our Saturday coverage pattern."

These masters come well prepared for weekend missions in slow moving vehicles armed with junk food, generic soda, oversized clothing, fanny packs, wide-brimmed hats, GPS devices and the rare gift to negotiate prices less than a dollar.

Items purchased at the sales are immediately sold at flea markets and online resellers for a profit or hoarded in homes for future generations or true crime TV show settings.

"I don't give sh** what they do with other people's crap," Mr. Kennedy responded when told of the popularity of the sales as he roped off his driveway. "Why would I invite a bunch of f***in' strangers to my house? These a**holes are still showing up!"

Veteran tagger Marcus Rutherford was none too pleased with the goings on at the Kennedy's as he smoked a butt, ignoring my assurance that there would be no tag sale today.

"Jackie and I were all set to start here as part of a busy day of tagging and we get this," he said, incredulously. "I don't know what's going on, but we were going to designate 20 minutes here and 15 to the next stop and now we've got to make adjustments on the fly all day. This world is going to hell in a hen basket."

I corrected his analogy to 'hell in a handbasket,' which still makes no sense, but his point was made.

Antonio Zaccaro, who backed his truck up the Kennedy driveway, intends to approach the Town to crack down on the tag sale ordinance in Burnham.

"We must have an ordinance for police to identify permitted tag sales," he stressed. "My assistant and I came here looking for *Wacky Packages*, *Partridge Family* and film memorabilia, as any tagger worth his salt would expect to find in a neighborhood like this."

Local artist Frankie Cabrera reasoned, "We just heard a minute ago that he didn't plan this sale, but since we're all here and traffic is backed up, can't he just pop open the garage and let us have a quick look?"

The ad in the local paper welcomed early birds and boasted of vintage clothing, musical instruments, HDTVs, vintage dishes, 70s memorabilia, classic furniture from the 50s and much more.

All anyone got was disappointment.

"I've been searching for a Hammond organ for the last ten years and I thought today might be my lucky day," said Topaz Swindell, a local poet in a surly mood, oblivious to the fact that there was no sale at the house. "Is he going to open that garage or am I going to have to open it for him?"

After several hours, police determined the announcement of the tag sale was a hoax concocted by an acquaintance of the Kennedy's, Rick Edmondson, bartender at the local Hard Times Tavern. He submitted the advertisements as an act of revenge toward the couple.

The Kennedys – both regulars at the tavern – allegedly stopped in for drinks earlier in the week and gave Edmondson another in a long series of extremely poor tips after spending several hours at the establishment.

"What comes around goes around," is all Edmondson reportedly said to police during questioning.

Mr. Kennedy declined to press charges, but Burnham Police Sergeant Jeff Casey confirmed that several of the taggers filed complaints. Asked how residents can prevent such scams in the future, Sergeant Casey offered only one bit of advice.

"Tip your bartender."

###

About the Author

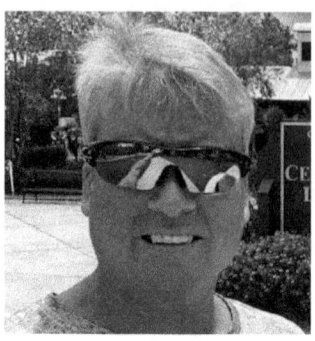

Bob Deakin has been a writer and journalist for the past 20 years, with more than 1,000 stories published, while working other jobs that may or may not have been a good fit. He grew up in Connecticut trying to look like a writer while wishing it were as warm and sunny as Florida, where he now resides.

Visit his website and blog at BobDeakin.com

www.ingramcontent.com/pod-product-compliance
Lightning Source LLC
Chambersburg PA
CBHW070642220526
45466CB00001B/259